See You Later, Mom!

FRANCES LINCOLN CHILDREN'S BOOKS

This book is for Amy, William, and Mike.
With grateful thanks to Footsteps, The Honey Pot,
and Heather Ridge Infants School
for all their help and support.

On Monday morning William went with his Mom
to preschool for the first time.
He was very excited.

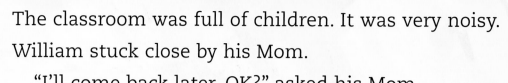

The classroom was full of children. It was very noisy.
William stuck close by his Mom.

"I'll come back later, OK?" asked his Mom.

"Can you stay?" asked William, feeling shy.

They watched the children painting, but William
didn't want to join in.

A little boy was sitting in a big truck in a corner.
He wasn't painting either.

"Did you have fun?" his Mom asked on the way home.
"I didn't feel like painting today," said William.

On Tuesday William went with his Mom to preschool.
"Should I come back later?" asked his Mom,
as she hung up his raincoat.
"No, please stay," said William.

So his Mom stayed.

The other children were singing songs and clapping.
William liked the clapping, but he didn't
know all the songs.

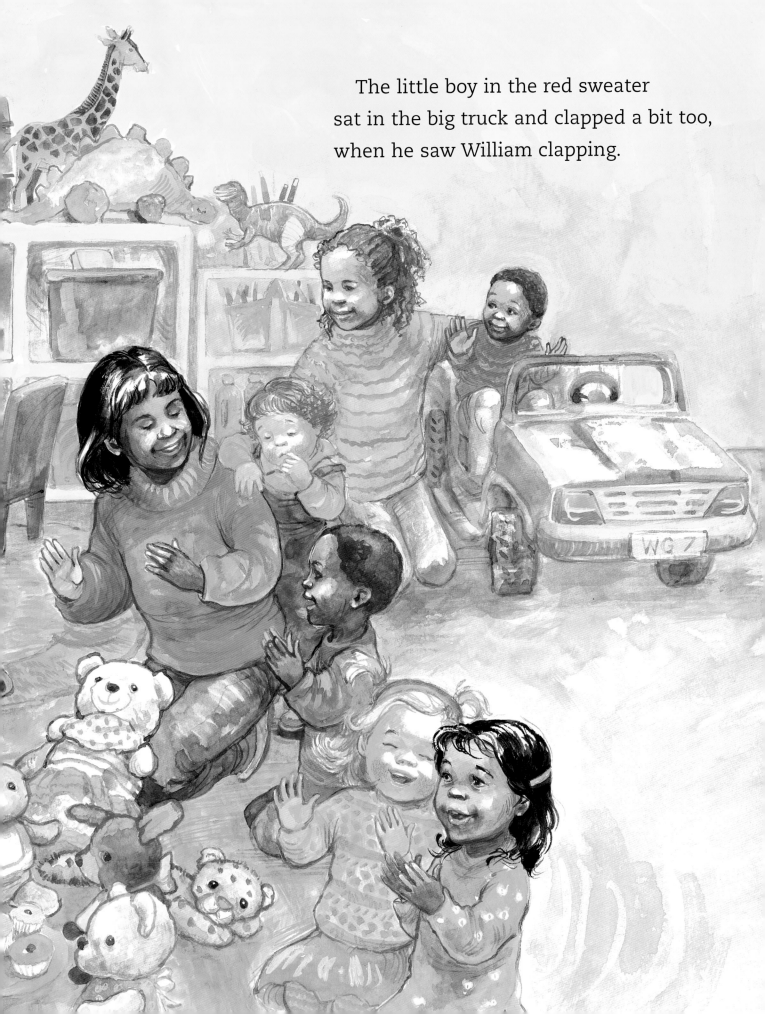

The little boy in the red sweater
sat in the big truck and clapped a bit too,
when he saw William clapping.

"Did you enjoy preschool today?" William's Mom asked on the way home.

"Well, I didn't feel like singing today," said William, "but the clapping was OK. That little boy in the truck didn't sing either."

On Wednesday morning William and his Mom went to preschool.
The teacher was very happy to see him.
"Should I come back later?" William's Mom asked, as she helped him
off with his boots.

The children were making playdough shapes,
cookies and snakes.

"Can you stay?" asked William.

So his Mom sat on a chair. William sat near the other
children, and played with some playdough too.

"Do you think that little boy would like some?" he asked his Mom.

"He might," she said. "Why don't you ask him?"

William went over to the boy and gave him
some of his playdough.

"Thank you," said the little boy, and rolled out
a long snake with it.

"Did you have fun today?" William's Mom asked on the way home.

"I made a good playdough truck," said William, "and that little boy made a snake. I think he liked me giving him some of mine."

"I think so too," she said. "Why don't you ask him what his name is tomorrow?"

On Thursday morning William and his Mom
went to preschool.
William was even looking forward to it a little bit.
"I'll see you later, OK?" his Mom asked,
putting William's lunch-box on the shelf.

The children were playing a jumping-up
and falling-down game.

"Please stay," said William. He didn't feel like
jumping up or falling down.

The little boy was sitting in the truck again.

William went over to him and asked him what his name was.

"David," said the boy, "what's yours?"

"William," said William. "Can you drive this truck?"

"Only outside," said David, "but it's too rainy to go out. It has to be a sunny day."

"How was preschool today?" William's Mom asked on the way home.

"It was OK," said William. "I've got a friend now. His name is David. He says he can drive that big truck, but only when it's not raining."

On Friday morning William couldn't wait
to get to preschool. The sun was shining.
When they arrived he took off his coat
and hung it up. He put his lunch-box on the shelf.

David was waiting for William in the truck.

William climbed in.

"Can we go outside today?" he asked the teacher.

She opened the big door, and all the children
pushed the truck into the playground.

"You can go home now, Mom!" called William.

"See you later!"

First published in Great Britain and in the USA in 2006
by Frances Lincoln Children's Books, 4 Torriano Mews,
Torriano Avenue, London NW5 2RZ

www.franceslincoln.com

Distributed in the USA by Publishers Group West

British Library Cataloguing in Publication Data
available on request

ISBN 1 84507 537 4

Printed in Singapore

9 8 7 6 5 4 3 2 1